Plants vs. Zombies

BULLY FOR YOU #2

ABDO
Spotlight

DARK
HORSE
COMICS

PopCap

Written by **PAUL TOBIN**
Art by **RON CHAN**
Colors by **MATTHEW J. RAINWATER**
Letters by **STEVE DUTRO**
Cover by **RON CHAN**

President and Publisher **MIKE RICHARDSON**
Editor **PHILIP R. SIMON**
Assistant Editor **ROXY POLK**
Designer **KAT LARSON**
Digital Production **CHRISTINA McKENZIE**

Special thanks to LEIGH BEACH, GARY CLAY, SHANA DOERR, A.J. RATHBUN, KRISTEN STAR, JEREMY VANHOOZER, and everyone at PopCap Games.

DarkHorse.com | PopCap.com

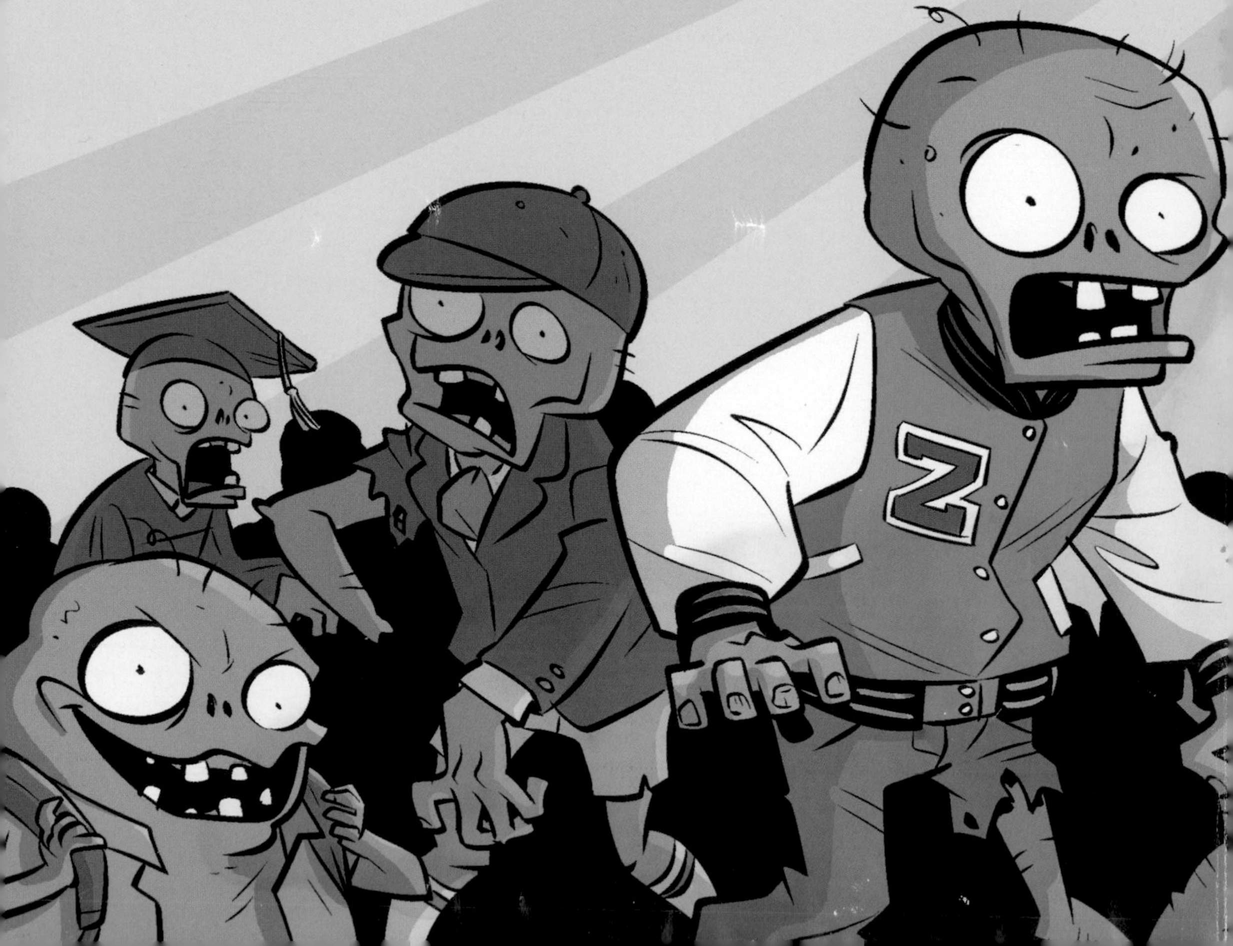
Z

PLANTS VS. ZOMBIES™

BULLY FOR YOU #2

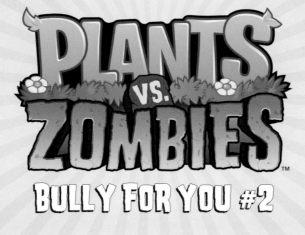

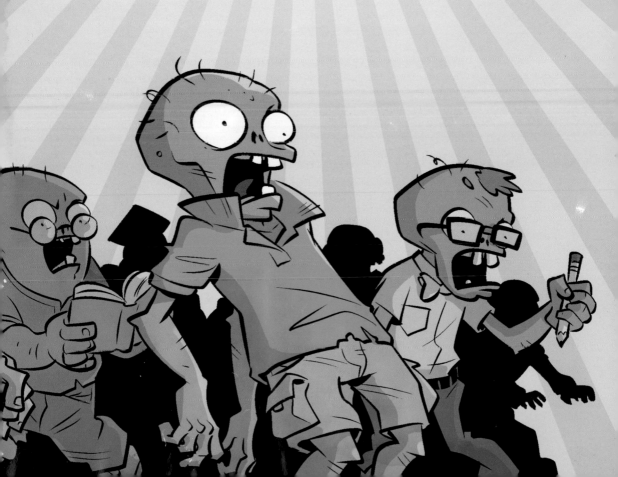

ABDOPUBLISHING.COM

Reinforced library bound edition published in 2017 by Spotlight, a division of ABDO, PO Box 398166, Minneapolis, Minnesota 55439. Spotlight produces high-quality reinforced library bound editions for schools and libraries.
Published by agreement with Dark Horse Comics.

Printed in the United States of America, North Mankato, Minnesota.
042016
092016

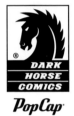

THIS BOOK CONTAINS RECYCLED MATERIALS

Originally issued as Plants vs. Zombies: Bully for You #2 by Dark Horse Comics in 2015.

PUBLISHER'S CATALOGING IN PUBLICATION DATA

Names: Tobin, Paul, author. | Chan, Ron ; Rainwater, Matthew J., illustrators.
Title: Bully for you / by Paul Tobin ; illustrated by Ron Chan and Matthew J. Rainwater.
Description: Minneapolis, MN : Spotlight, [2017] | Series: Plants vs. zombies
Summary: Caught in the middle of zombie warfare, Nate and Patrice must join forces with Crazy Dave to beat them but could Crazy Dave's ice cream obsession save the day?
Identifiers: LCCN 2016934735 | ISBN 9781614795346 (v.1 : lib. bdg.) | ISBN 9781614795353 (v.2 : lib. bdg.) | ISBN 9781614795360 (v.3 : lib. bdg.)
Subjects: LCSH: Bullying--Juvenile fiction. | Plants--Juvenile fiction. | Zombies--Juvenile fiction. | Adventure and adventurers--Juvenile fiction. | Comic books strips, etc.--Juvenile fiction. | Graphic novels--Juvenile fiction.
Classification: DDC 741.5--dc23
LC record available at http://lccn.loc.gov/2016934735

Spotlight

A Division of ABDO
abdopublishing.com

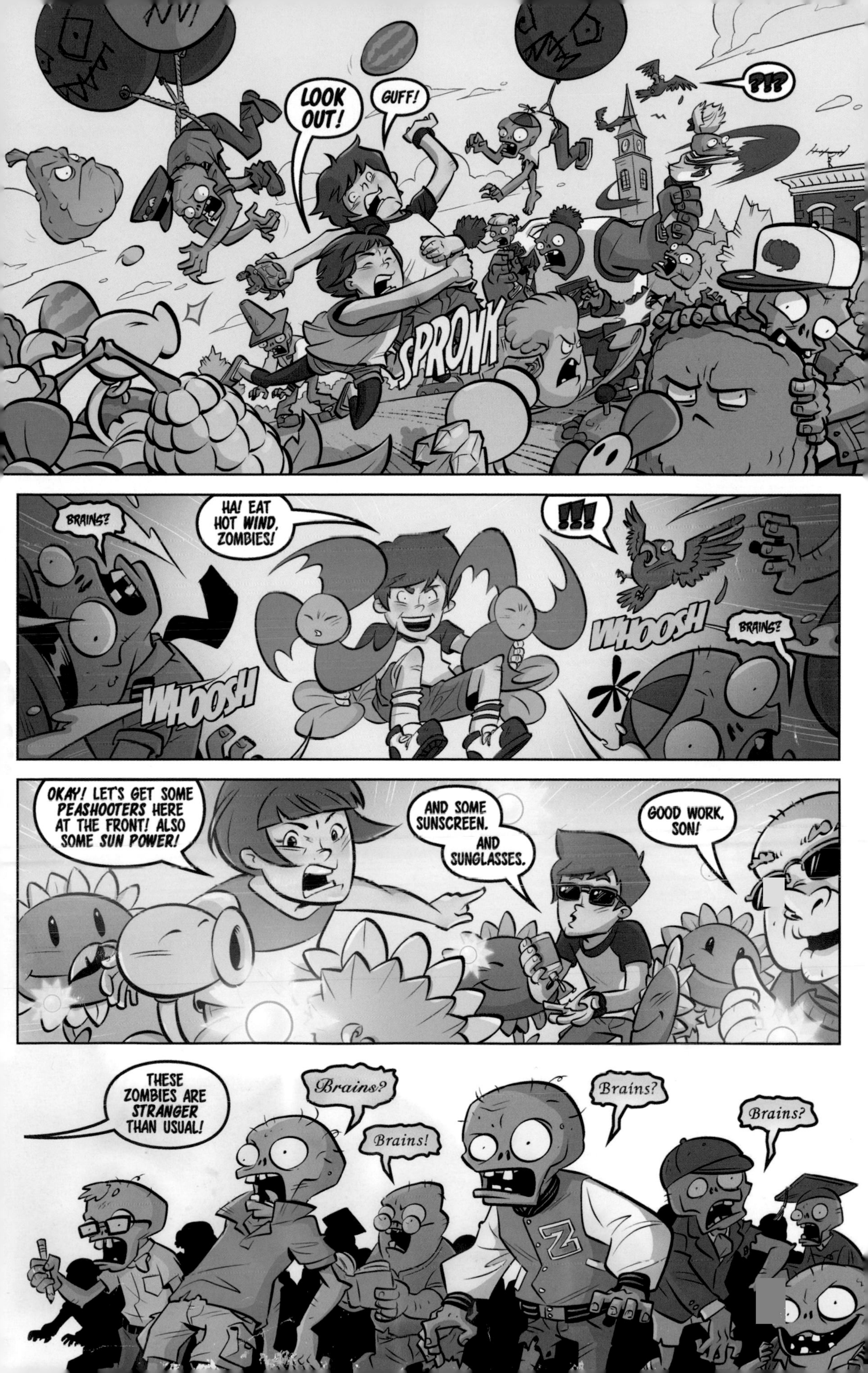
LOOK OUT!
GUFF!
??
SPRONK
BRAINS?
HA! EAT HOT WIND, ZOMBIES!
!!!
WHOOSH
WHOOSH
BRAINS?
OKAY! LET'S GET SOME PEASHOOTERS HERE AT THE FRONT! ALSO SOME SUN POWER!
AND SOME SUNSCREEN.
AND SUNGLASSES.
GOOD WORK, SON!
THESE ZOMBIES ARE STRANGER THAN USUAL!
Brains?
Brains!
Brains?
Brains?

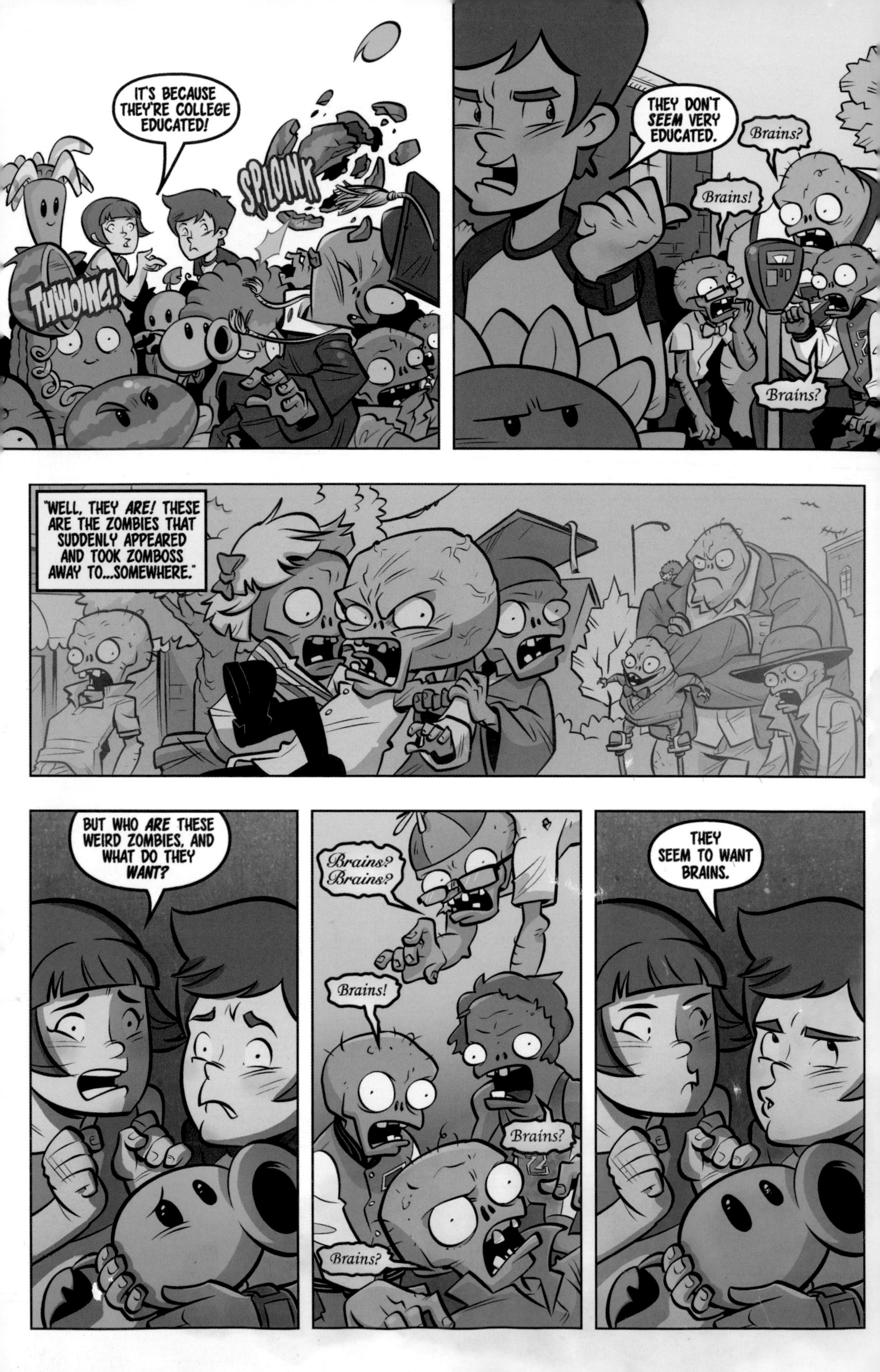
IT'S BECAUSE THEY'RE COLLEGE EDUCATED!
SPLOINK
THWOING!
THEY DON'T SEEM VERY EDUCATED.
Brains?
Brains!
Brains?
"WELL, THEY ARE! THESE ARE THE ZOMBIES THAT SUDDENLY APPEARED AND TOOK ZOMBOSS AWAY TO...SOMEWHERE."
BUT WHO ARE THESE WEIRD ZOMBIES, AND WHAT DO THEY WANT?
Brains? Brains?
Brains!
Brains?
Brains?
THEY SEEM TO WANT BRAINS.

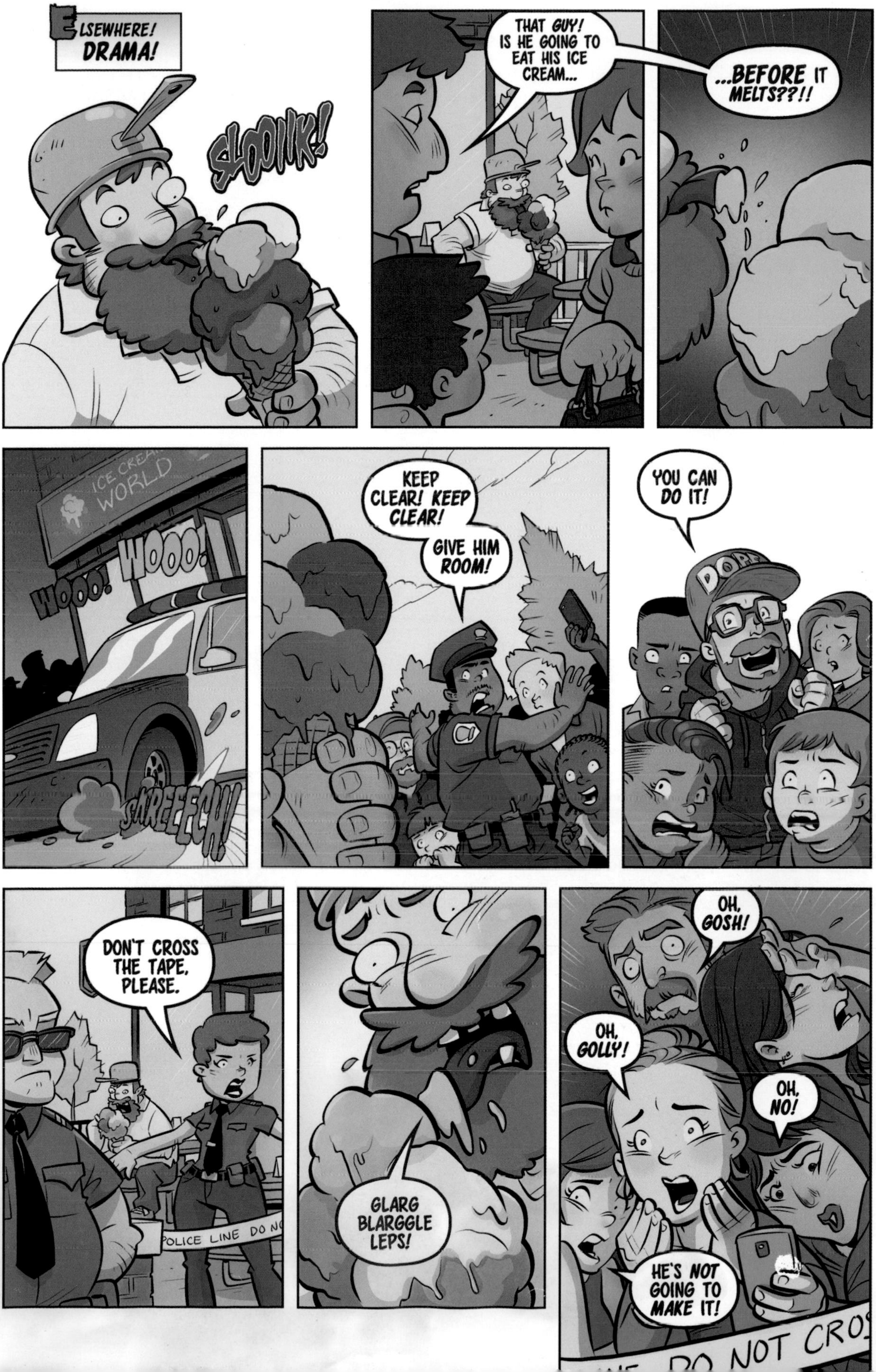
ELSEWHERE! DRAMA!
SLOOIIK!
THAT GUY! IS HE GOING TO EAT HIS ICE CREAM...
...BEFORE IT MELTS??!!
ICE CREAM WORLD
WOOO! WOOO!
SKREEECH!
KEEP CLEAR! KEEP CLEAR!
GIVE HIM ROOM!
YOU CAN DO IT!
DON'T CROSS THE TAPE, PLEASE.
POLICE LINE DO NO
GLARG BLARGGLE LEPS!
OH, GOSH!
OH, GOLLY!
OH, NO!
HE'S NOT GOING TO MAKE IT!
DO NOT CROS

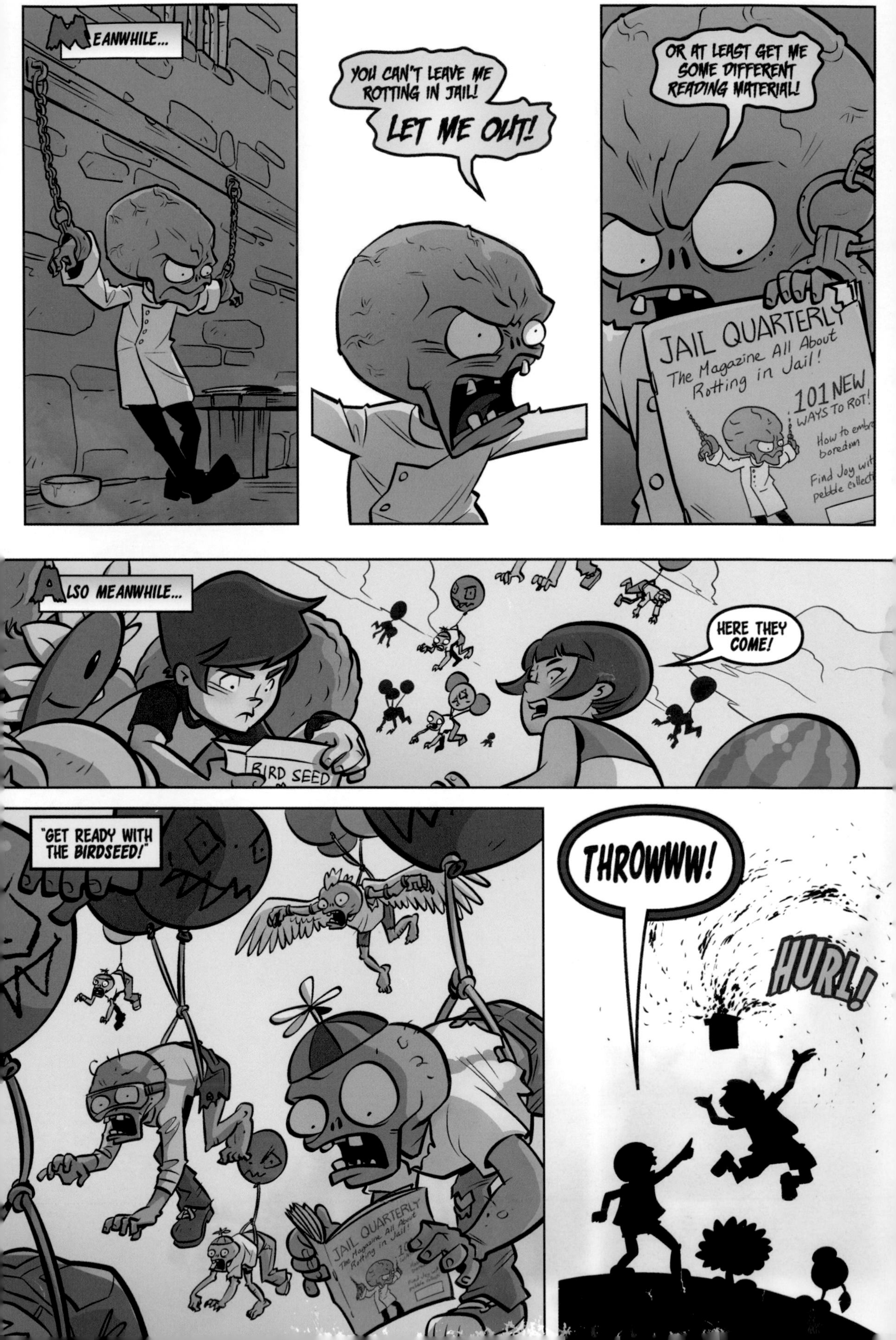
MEANWHILE...
YOU CAN'T LEAVE ME ROTTING IN JAIL!
LET ME OUT!
OR AT LEAST GET ME SOME DIFFERENT READING MATERIAL!
JAIL QUARTERLY
The Magazine All About Rotting in Jail!
101 NEW WAYS TO ROT!
How to embra
boredom
Find Joy wit
pebble collect
ALSO MEANWHILE...
HERE THEY COME!
BIRD SEED
"GET READY WITH THE BIRDSEED!"
JAIL QUARTERLY
The Magazine All About Rotting in Jail!
THROWWW!
HURL!

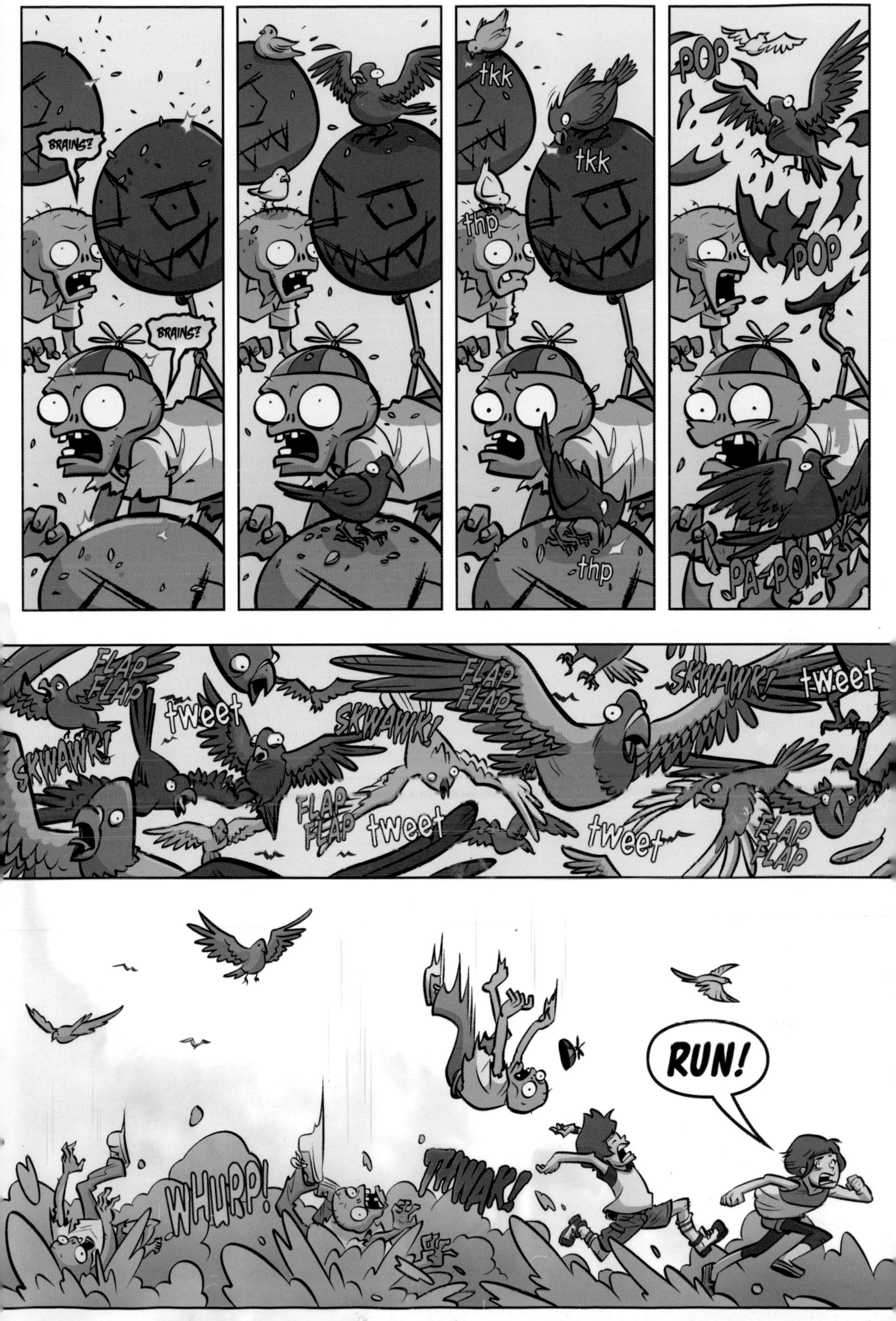
BRAINS?
BRAINS?
tkk
tkk
thp
thp
POP
POP
PA-POP!
FLAP FLAP
tweet
SKWAWK!
SKWAWK!
FLAP FLAP
SKWAWK!
tweet
FLAP FLAP
tweet
tweet
FLAP FLAP
WHUPP!
THWAK!
RUN!

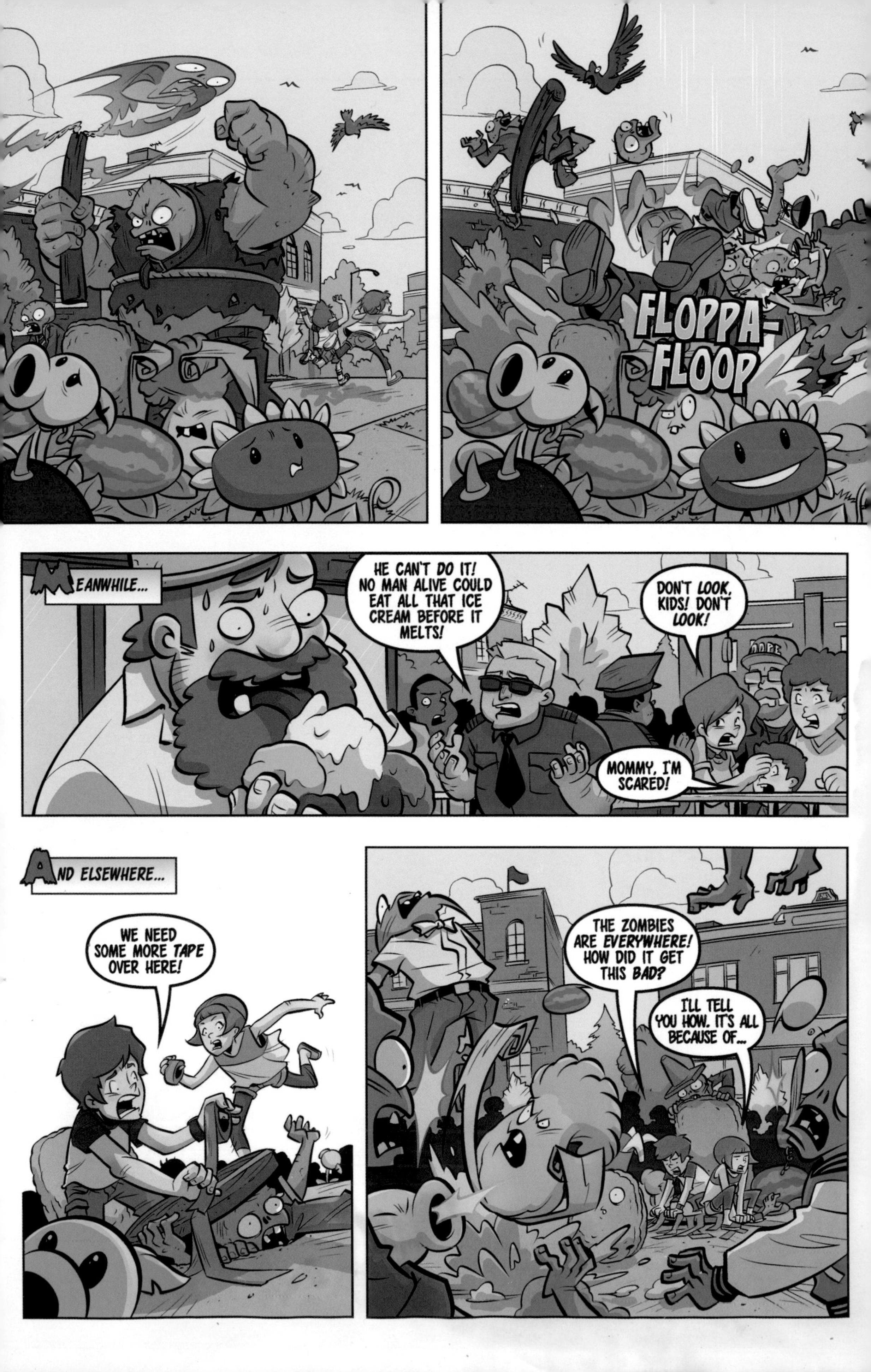
FLOPPA-FLOOP
MEANWHILE...
HE CAN'T DO IT! NO MAN ALIVE COULD EAT ALL THAT ICE CREAM BEFORE IT MELTS!
DON'T LOOK, KIDS! DON'T LOOK!
MOMMY, I'M SCARED!
AND ELSEWHERE...
WE NEED SOME MORE TAPE OVER HERE!
THE ZOMBIES ARE EVERYWHERE! HOW DID IT GET THIS BAD?
I'LL TELL YOU HOW. IT'S ALL BECAUSE OF...

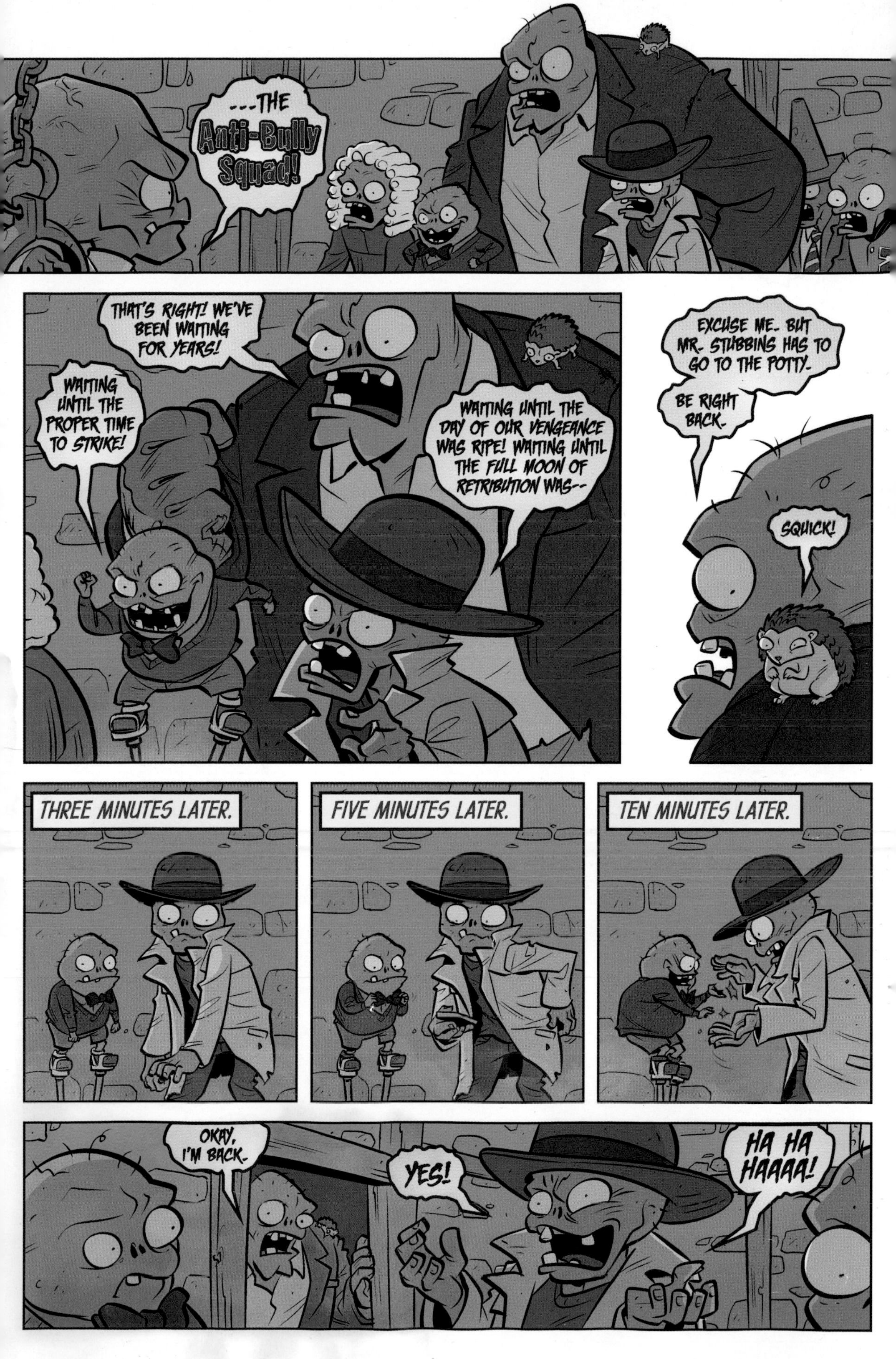
...THE Anti-Bully Squad!
THAT'S RIGHT! WE'VE BEEN WAITING FOR YEARS!
WAITING UNTIL THE PROPER TIME TO STRIKE!
WAITING UNTIL THE DAY OF OUR VENGEANCE WAS RIPE! WAITING UNTIL THE FULL MOON OF RETRIBUTION WAS--
EXCUSE ME.. BUT MR. STUBBINS HAS TO GO TO THE POTTY.
BE RIGHT BACK.
SQUICK!
THREE MINUTES LATER.
FIVE MINUTES LATER.
TEN MINUTES LATER.
OKAY, I'M BACK.
YES!
HA HA HAAAA!

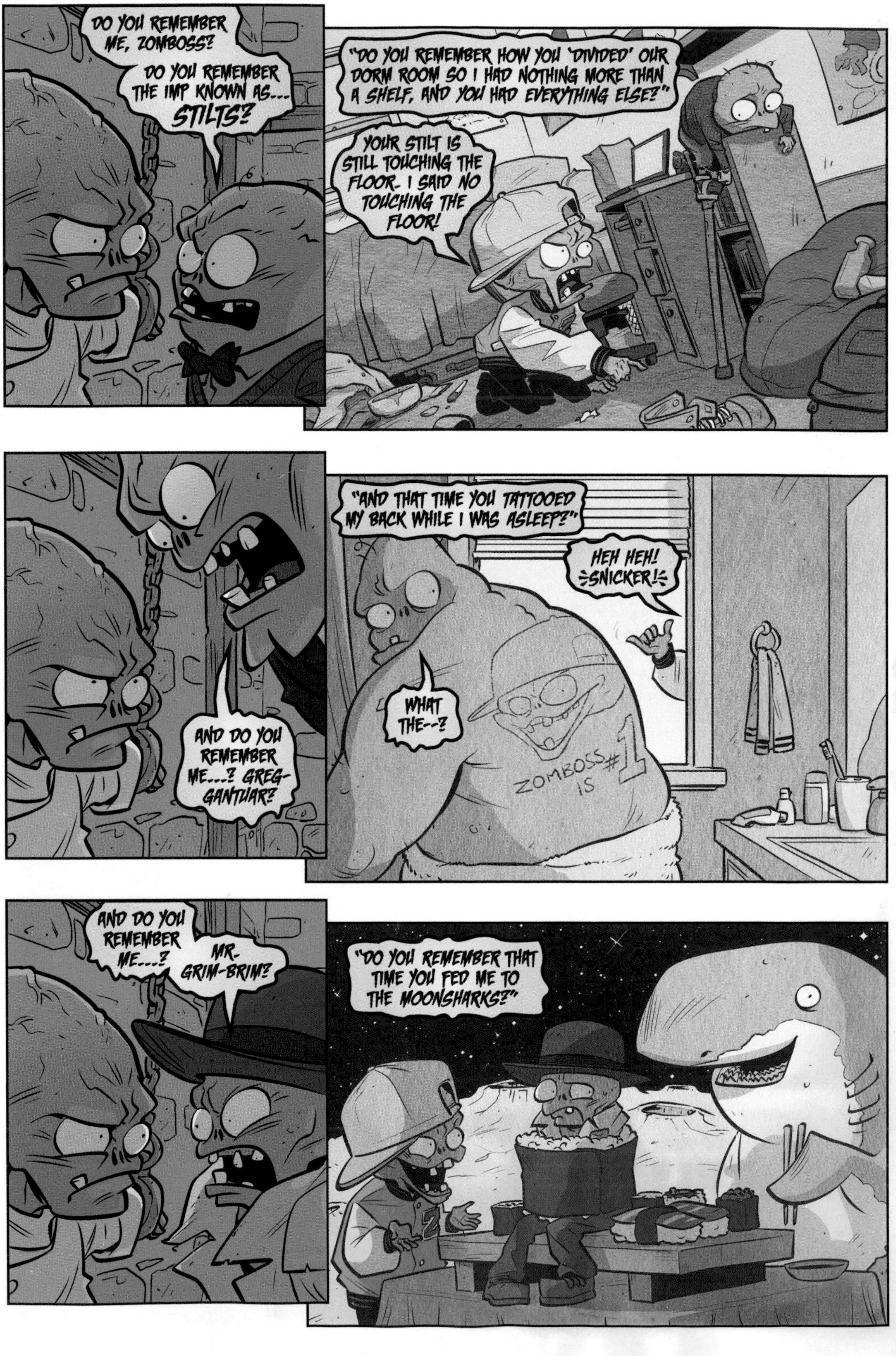
DO YOU REMEMBER ME, ZOMBOSS?
DO YOU REMEMBER THE IMP KNOWN AS... STILTS?
"DO YOU REMEMBER HOW YOU 'DIVIDED' OUR DORM ROOM SO I HAD NOTHING MORE THAN A SHELF, AND YOU HAD EVERYTHING ELSE?"
YOUR STILT IS STILL TOUCHING THE FLOOR. I SAID NO TOUCHING THE FLOOR!
AND DO YOU REMEMBER ME...? GREG-GANTUAR?
"AND THAT TIME YOU TATTOOED MY BACK WHILE I WAS ASLEEP?"
HEH HEH! SNICKER!
WHAT THE--?
ZOMBOSS IS #1
AND DO YOU REMEMBER ME...?
MR. GRIM-BRIM?
"DO YOU REMEMBER THAT TIME YOU FED ME TO THE MOONSHARKS?"

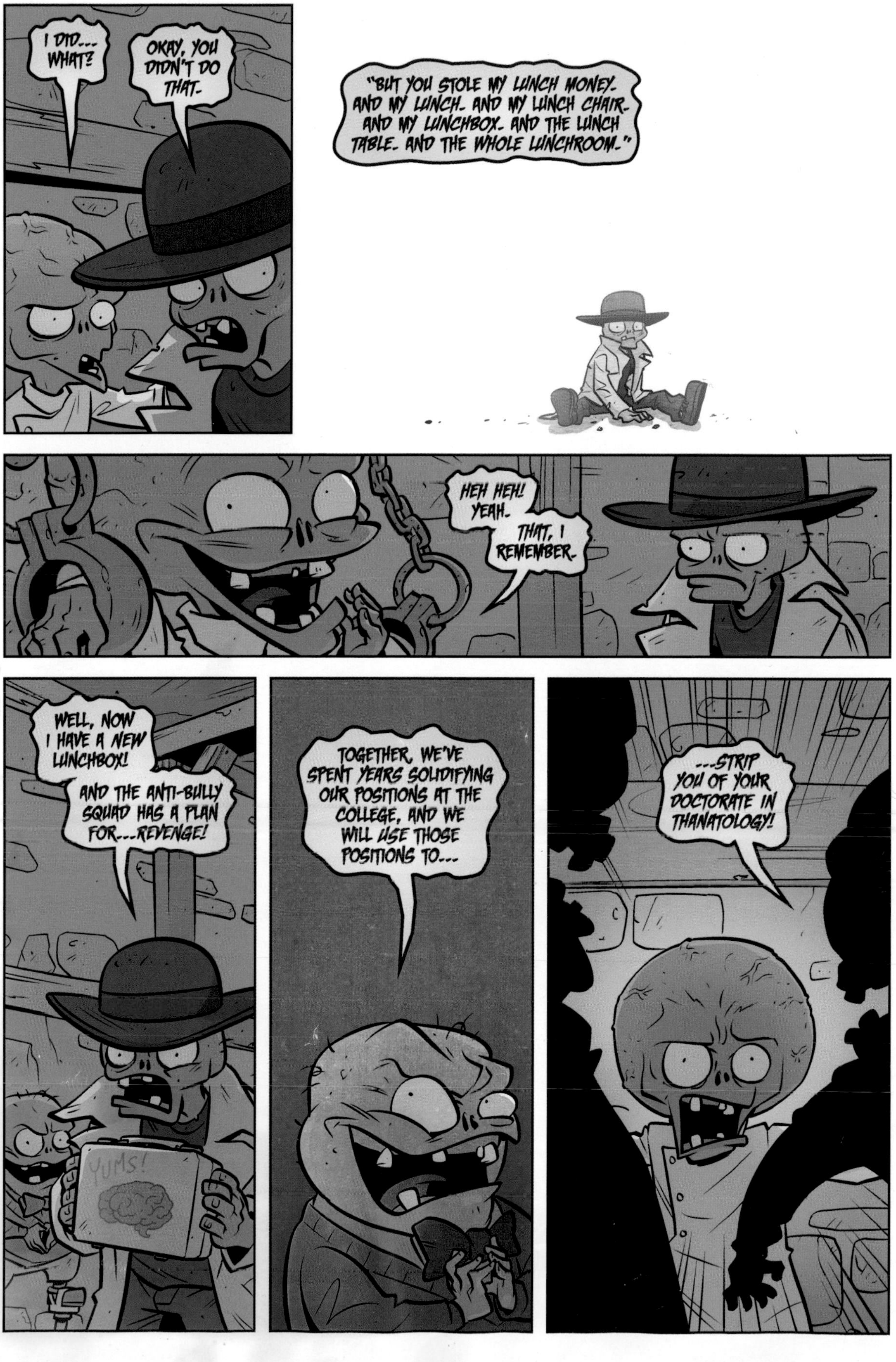
I DID... WHAT?
OKAY, YOU DIDN'T DO THAT.
"BUT YOU STOLE MY LUNCH MONEY. AND MY LUNCH. AND MY LUNCH CHAIR. AND MY LUNCHBOX. AND THE LUNCH TABLE. AND THE WHOLE LUNCHROOM."
HEH HEH! YEAH.
THAT, I REMEMBER.
WELL, NOW I HAVE A NEW LUNCHBOX!
AND THE ANTI-BULLY SQUAD HAS A PLAN FOR...REVENGE!
YUMS!
TOGETHER, WE'VE SPENT YEARS SOLIDIFYING OUR POSITIONS AT THE COLLEGE, AND WE WILL USE THOSE POSITIONS TO...
...STRIP YOU OF YOUR DOCTORATE IN THANATOLOGY!

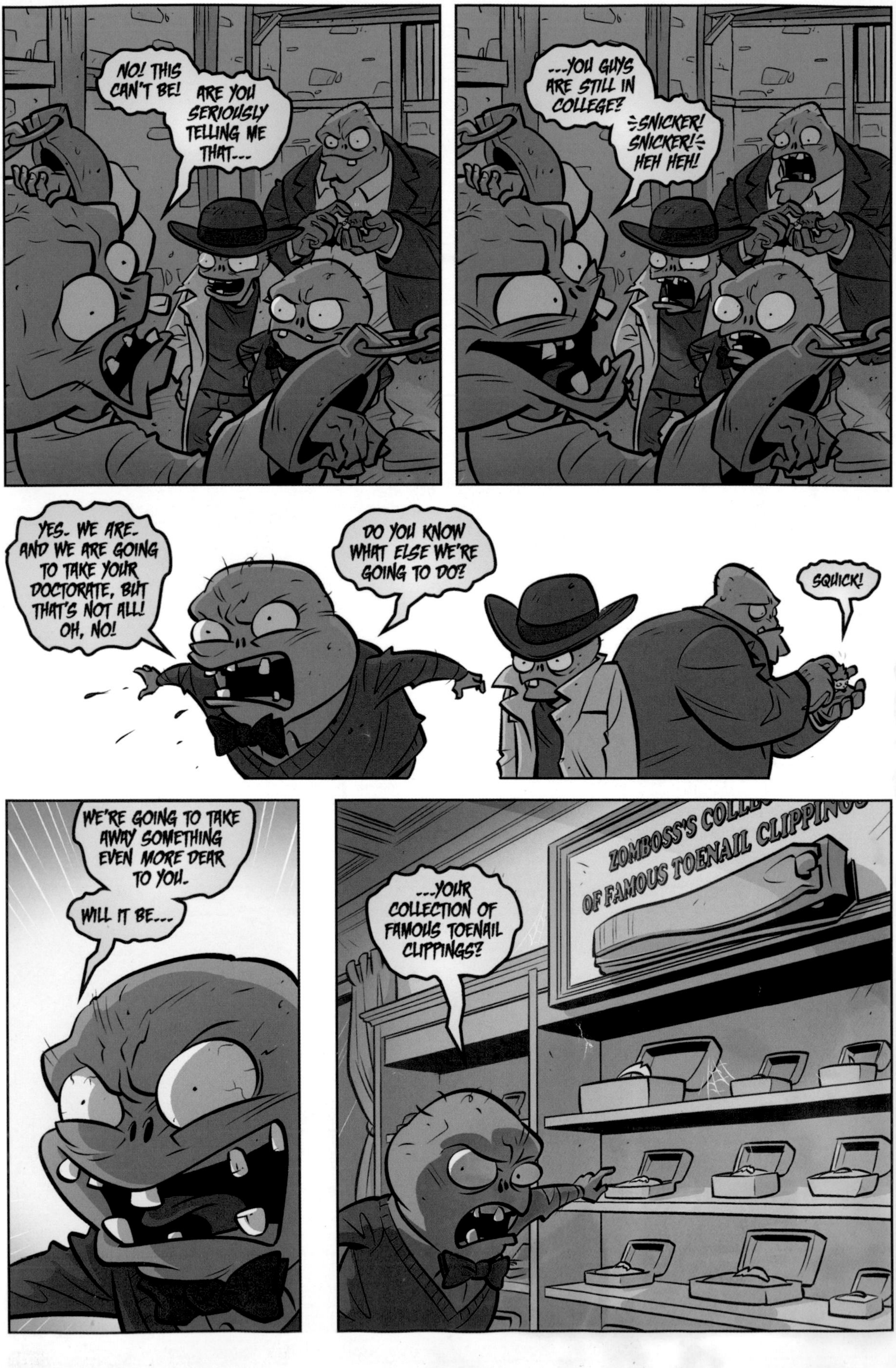
NO! THIS CAN'T BE!
ARE YOU SERIOUSLY TELLING ME THAT...
...YOU GUYS ARE STILL IN COLLEGE?
SNICKER! SNICKER! HEH HEH!
YES. WE ARE. AND WE ARE GOING TO TAKE YOUR DOCTORATE, BUT THAT'S NOT ALL! OH, NO!
DO YOU KNOW WHAT ELSE WE'RE GOING TO DO?
SQUICK!
WE'RE GOING TO TAKE AWAY SOMETHING EVEN MORE DEAR TO YOU.
WILL IT BE...
...YOUR COLLECTION OF FAMOUS TOENAIL CLIPPINGS?
ZOMBOSS'S COLLE
OF FAMOUS TOENAIL CLIPPINGS

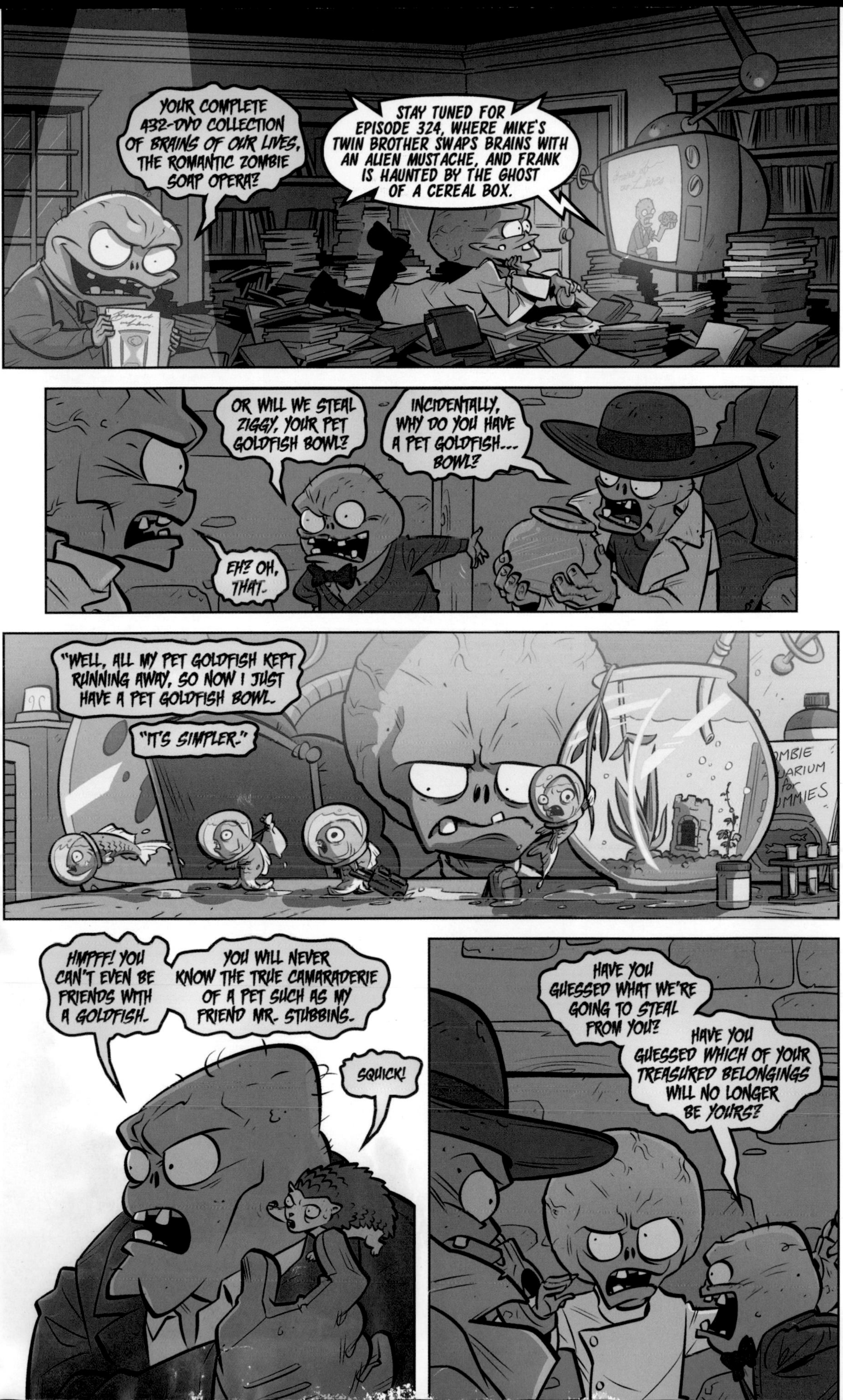
YOUR COMPLETE 432-DVD COLLECTION OF BRAINS OF OUR LIVES, THE ROMANTIC ZOMBIE SOAP OPERA?
STAY TUNED FOR EPISODE 324, WHERE MIKE'S TWIN BROTHER SWAPS BRAINS WITH AN ALIEN MUSTACHE, AND FRANK IS HAUNTED BY THE GHOST OF A CEREAL BOX.
OR WILL WE STEAL ZIGGY, YOUR PET GOLDFISH BOWL?
INCIDENTALLY, WHY DO YOU HAVE A PET GOLDFISH... BOWL?
EH? OH, THAT.
"WELL, ALL MY PET GOLDFISH KEPT RUNNING AWAY, SO NOW I JUST HAVE A PET GOLDFISH BOWL.
"IT'S SIMPLER."
HMPFF! YOU CAN'T EVEN BE FRIENDS WITH A GOLDFISH.
YOU WILL NEVER KNOW THE TRUE CAMARADERIE OF A PET SUCH AS MY FRIEND MR. STUBBINS.
SQUICK!
HAVE YOU GUESSED WHAT WE'RE GOING TO STEAL FROM YOU?
HAVE YOU GUESSED WHICH OF YOUR TREASURED BELONGINGS WILL NO LONGER BE YOURS?

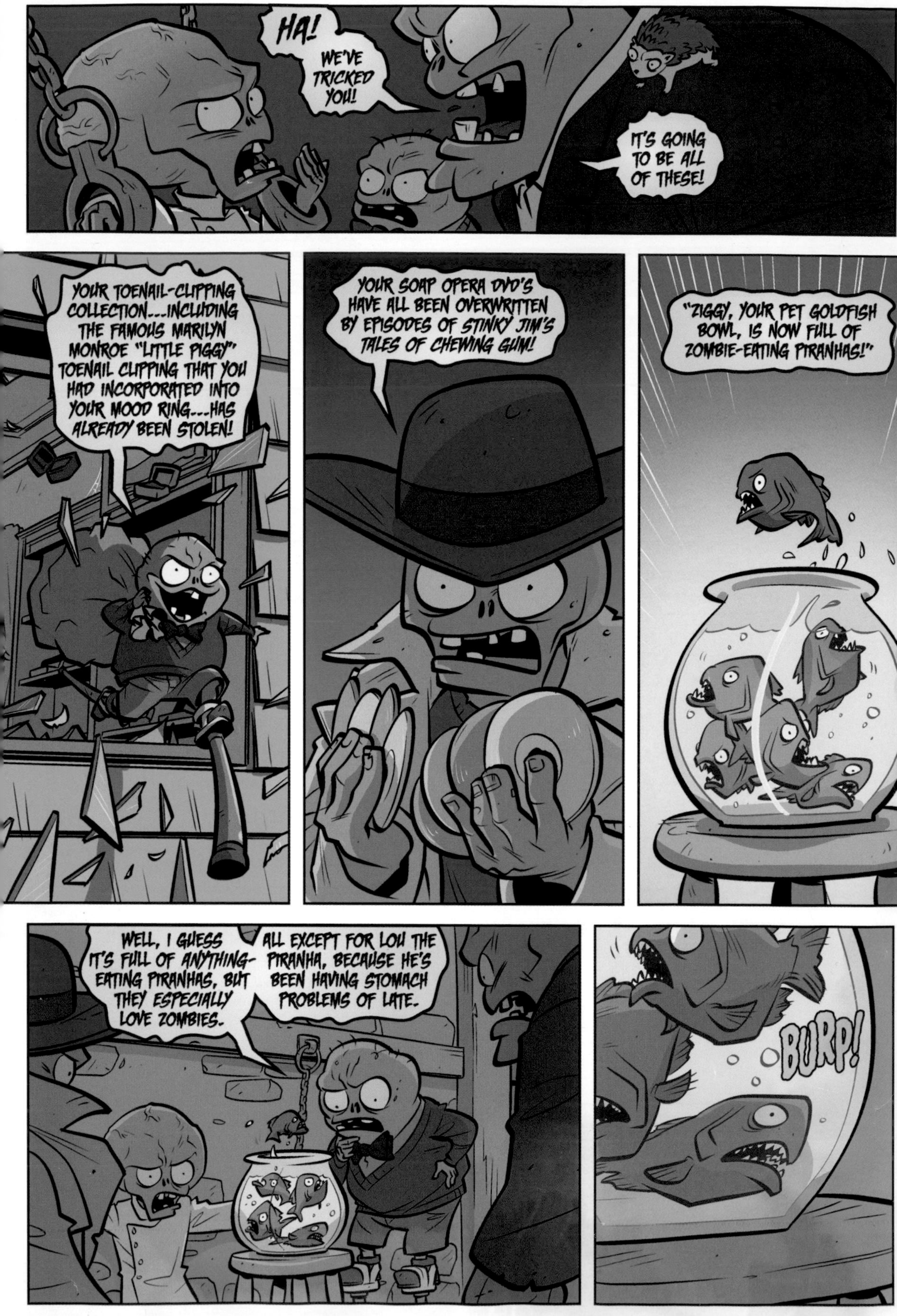
HA!
WE'VE TRICKED YOU!
IT'S GOING TO BE ALL OF THESE!
YOUR TOENAIL-CLIPPING COLLECTION...INCLUDING THE FAMOUS MARILYN MONROE "LITTLE PIGGY" TOENAIL CLIPPING THAT YOU HAD INCORPORATED INTO YOUR MOOD RING...HAS ALREADY BEEN STOLEN!
YOUR SOAP OPERA DVD'S HAVE ALL BEEN OVERWRITTEN BY EPISODES OF STINKY JIM'S TALES OF CHEWING GUM!
"ZIGGY, YOUR PET GOLDFISH BOWL, IS NOW FULL OF ZOMBIE-EATING PIRANHAS!"
WELL, I GUESS IT'S FULL OF ANYTHING-EATING PIRANHAS, BUT THEY ESPECIALLY LOVE ZOMBIES.
ALL EXCEPT FOR LOU THE PIRANHA, BECAUSE HE'S BEEN HAVING STOMACH PROBLEMS OF LATE.
BURP!

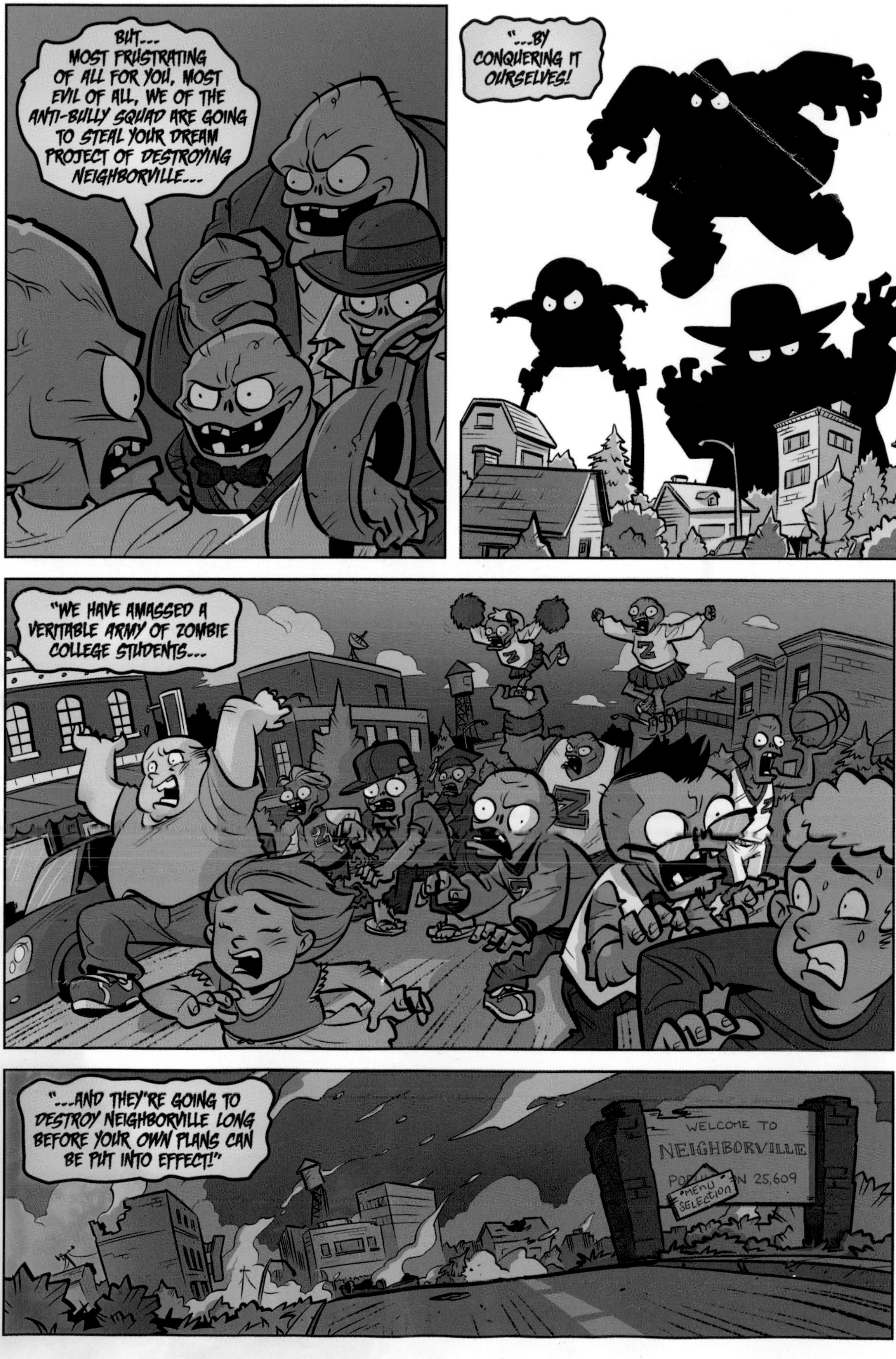
BUT... MOST FRUSTRATING OF ALL FOR YOU, MOST EVIL OF ALL, WE OF THE ANTI-BULLY SQUAD ARE GOING TO STEAL YOUR DREAM PROJECT OF DESTROYING NEIGHBORVILLE...
"...BY CONQUERING IT OURSELVES!
"WE HAVE AMASSED A VERITABLE ARMY OF ZOMBIE COLLEGE STUDENTS...
"...AND THEY'RE GOING TO DESTROY NEIGHBORVILLE LONG BEFORE YOUR OWN PLANS CAN BE PUT INTO EFFECT!"
WELCOME TO
NEIGHBORVILLE
N 25,609
MENU SELECTION

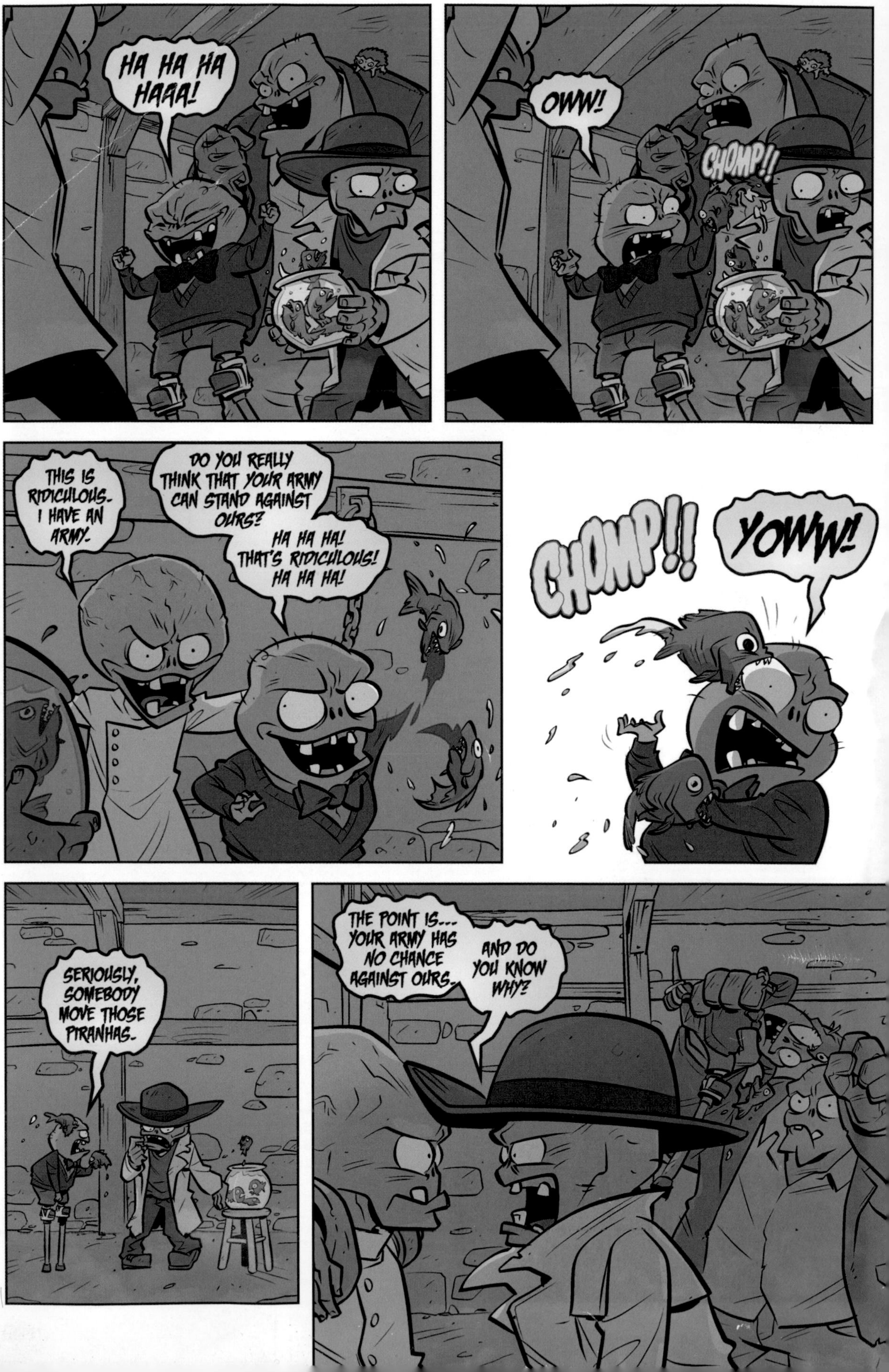
HA HA HA HAAA!
OWW!
CHOMP!!
THIS IS RIDICULOUS. I HAVE AN ARMY.
DO YOU REALLY THINK THAT YOUR ARMY CAN STAND AGAINST OURS?
HA HA HA! THAT'S RIDICULOUS! HA HA HA!
CHOMP!!
YOWW!
SERIOUSLY, SOMEBODY MOVE THOSE PIRANHAS.
THE POINT IS... YOUR ARMY HAS NO CHANCE AGAINST OURS.
AND DO YOU KNOW WHY?

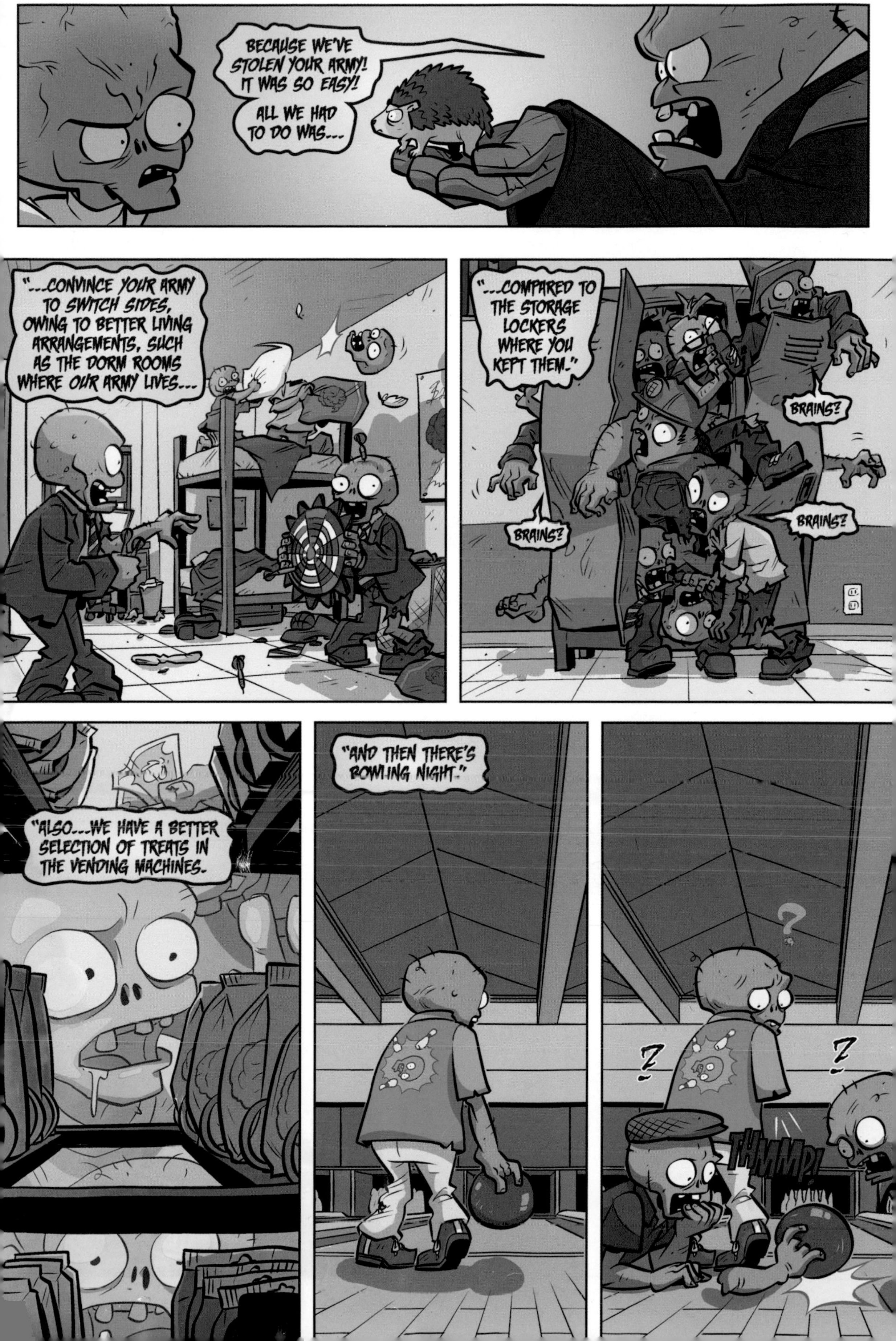
BECAUSE WE'VE STOLEN YOUR ARMY! IT WAS SO EASY!
ALL WE HAD TO DO WAS...
"...CONVINCE YOUR ARMY TO SWITCH SIDES, OWING TO BETTER LIVING ARRANGEMENTS, SUCH AS THE DORM ROOMS WHERE OUR ARMY LIVES...
"...COMPARED TO THE STORAGE LOCKERS WHERE YOU KEPT THEM."
BRAINS?
BRAINS?
BRAINS?
"ALSO...WE HAVE A BETTER SELECTION OF TREATS IN THE VENDING MACHINES.
"AND THEN THERE'S BOWLING NIGHT."
?
Z
Z
THMMP!

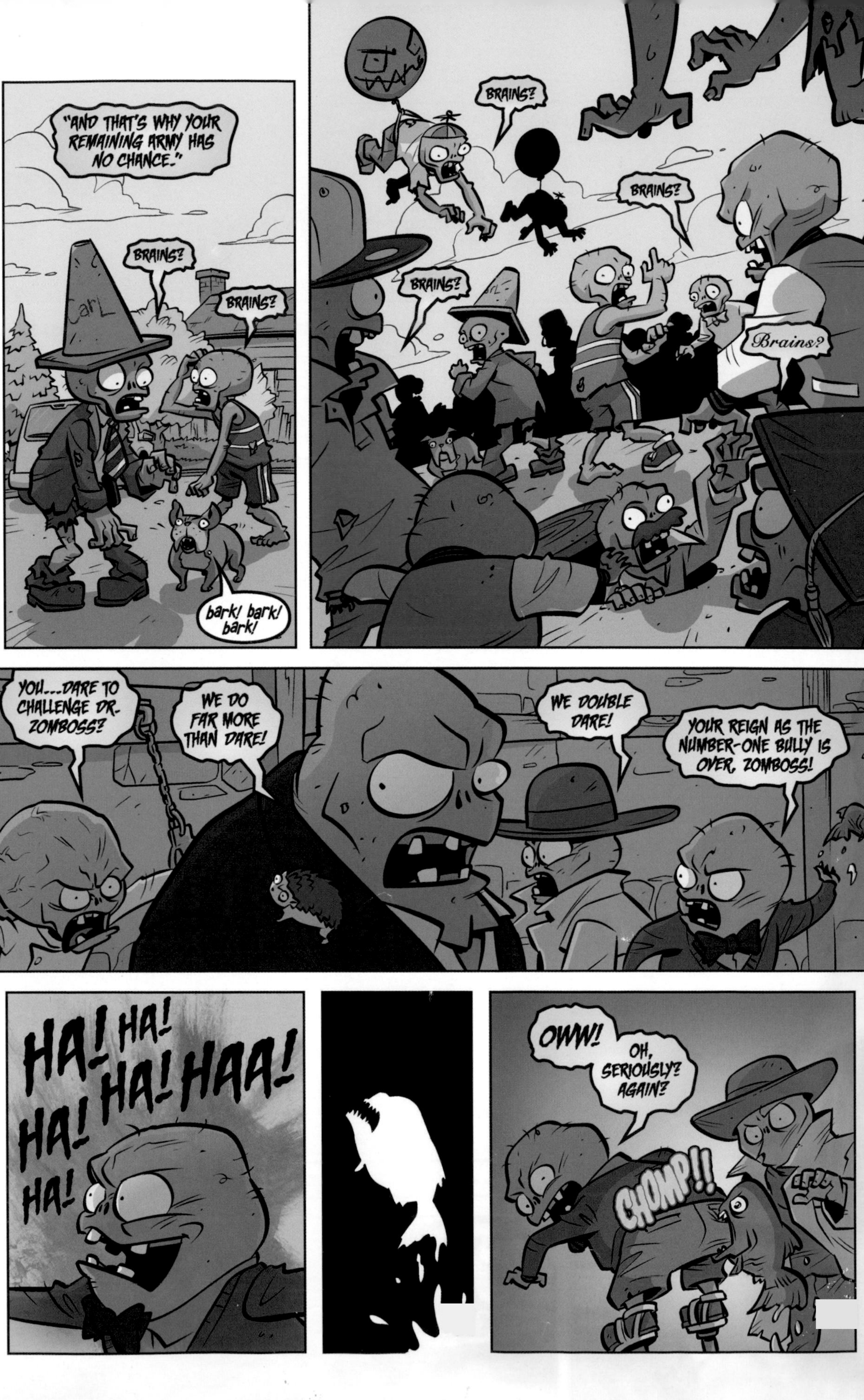
"AND THAT'S WHY YOUR REMAINING ARMY HAS NO CHANCE."
BRAINS?
BRAINS?
bark! bark! bark!
BRAINS?
BRAINS?
BRAINS?
Brains?
YOU...DARE TO CHALLENGE DR. ZOMBOSS?
WE DO FAR MORE THAN DARE!
WE DOUBLE DARE!
YOUR REIGN AS THE NUMBER-ONE BULLY IS OVER, ZOMBOSS!
HA! HA! HA! HA! HAA! HA!
OWW!
OH, SERIOUSLY? AGAIN?
CHOMP!!

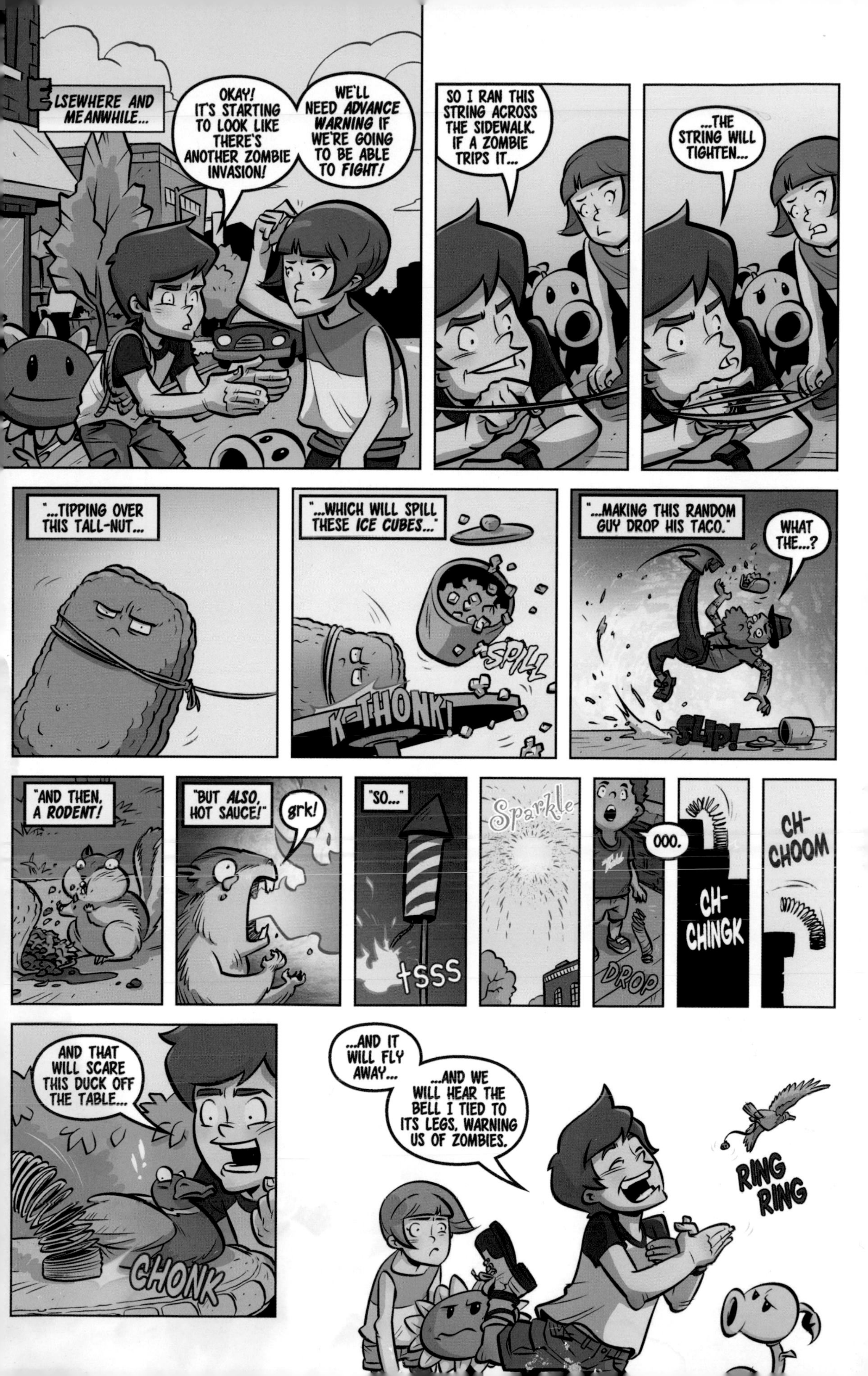

ELSEWHERE AND MEANWHILE...
OKAY! IT'S STARTING TO LOOK LIKE THERE'S ANOTHER ZOMBIE INVASION!
WE'LL NEED ADVANCE WARNING IF WE'RE GOING TO BE ABLE TO FIGHT!
SO I RAN THIS STRING ACROSS THE SIDEWALK. IF A ZOMBIE TRIPS IT...
...THE STRING WILL TIGHTEN...
"...TIPPING OVER THIS TALL-NUT...
"...WHICH WILL SPILL THESE ICE CUBES..."
SPILL
K-THONK!
"...MAKING THIS RANDOM GUY DROP HIS TACO."
WHAT THE...?
SLIP!
"AND THEN, A RODENT!
"BUT ALSO, HOT SAUCE!"
grk!
"SO..."
tsss
Sparkle
OOO.
DROP
CH-CHINGK
CH-CHOOM
AND THAT WILL SCARE THIS DUCK OFF THE TABLE...
CHONK
...AND IT WILL FLY AWAY...
...AND WE WILL HEAR THE BELL I TIED TO ITS LEGS, WARNING US OF ZOMBIES.
RING RING

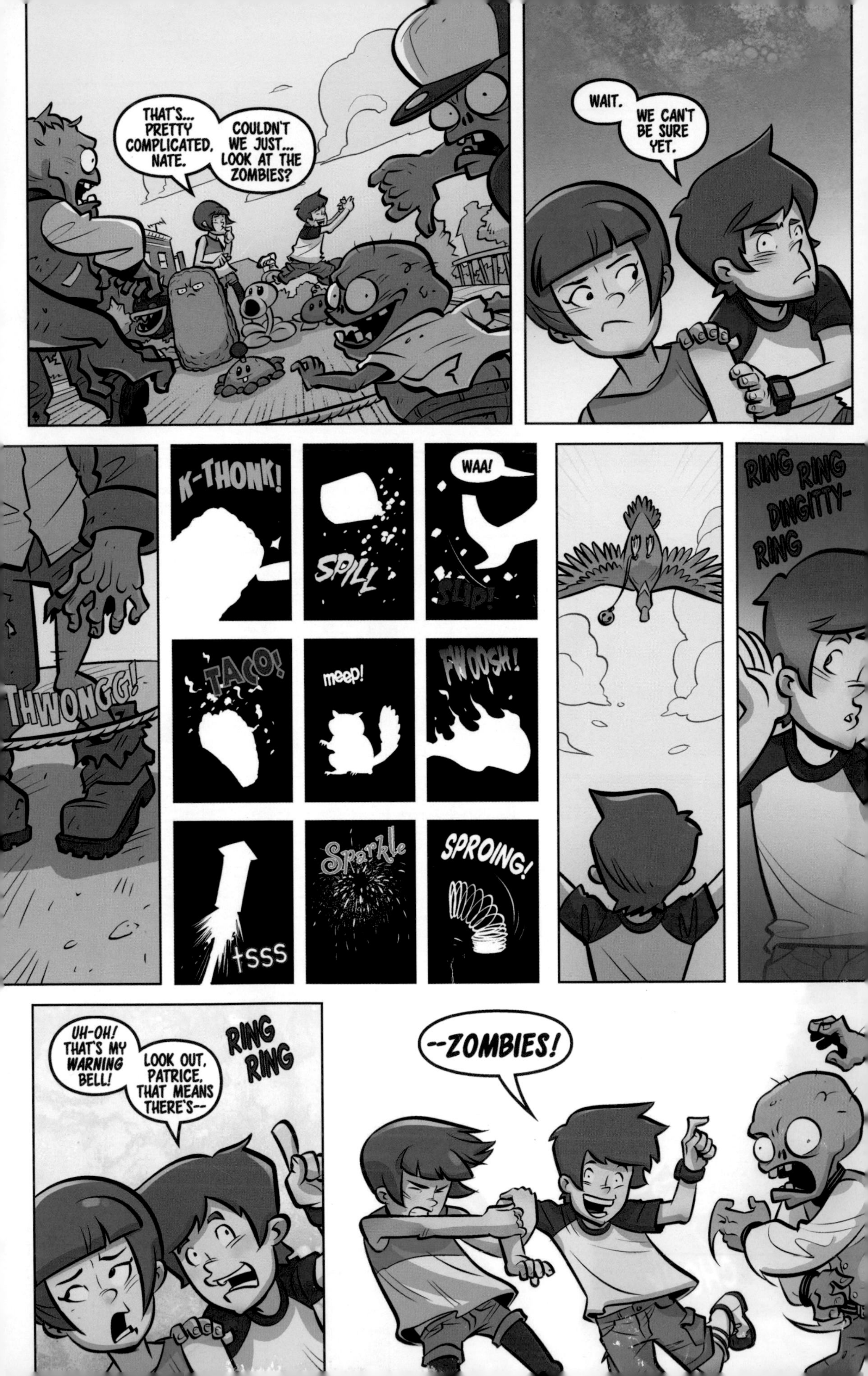
THAT'S... PRETTY COMPLICATED, NATE.
COULDN'T WE JUST... LOOK AT THE ZOMBIES?
WAIT. WE CAN'T BE SURE YET.
THWONGG!
K-THONK!
SPILL
WAA!
SLIP!
TACO!
meep!
FWOOSH!
tsss
Sparkle
SPROING!
RING RING DINGITTY-RING
UH-OH! THAT'S MY WARNING BELL!
LOOK OUT, PATRICE, THAT MEANS THERE'S--
RING RING
--ZOMBIES!

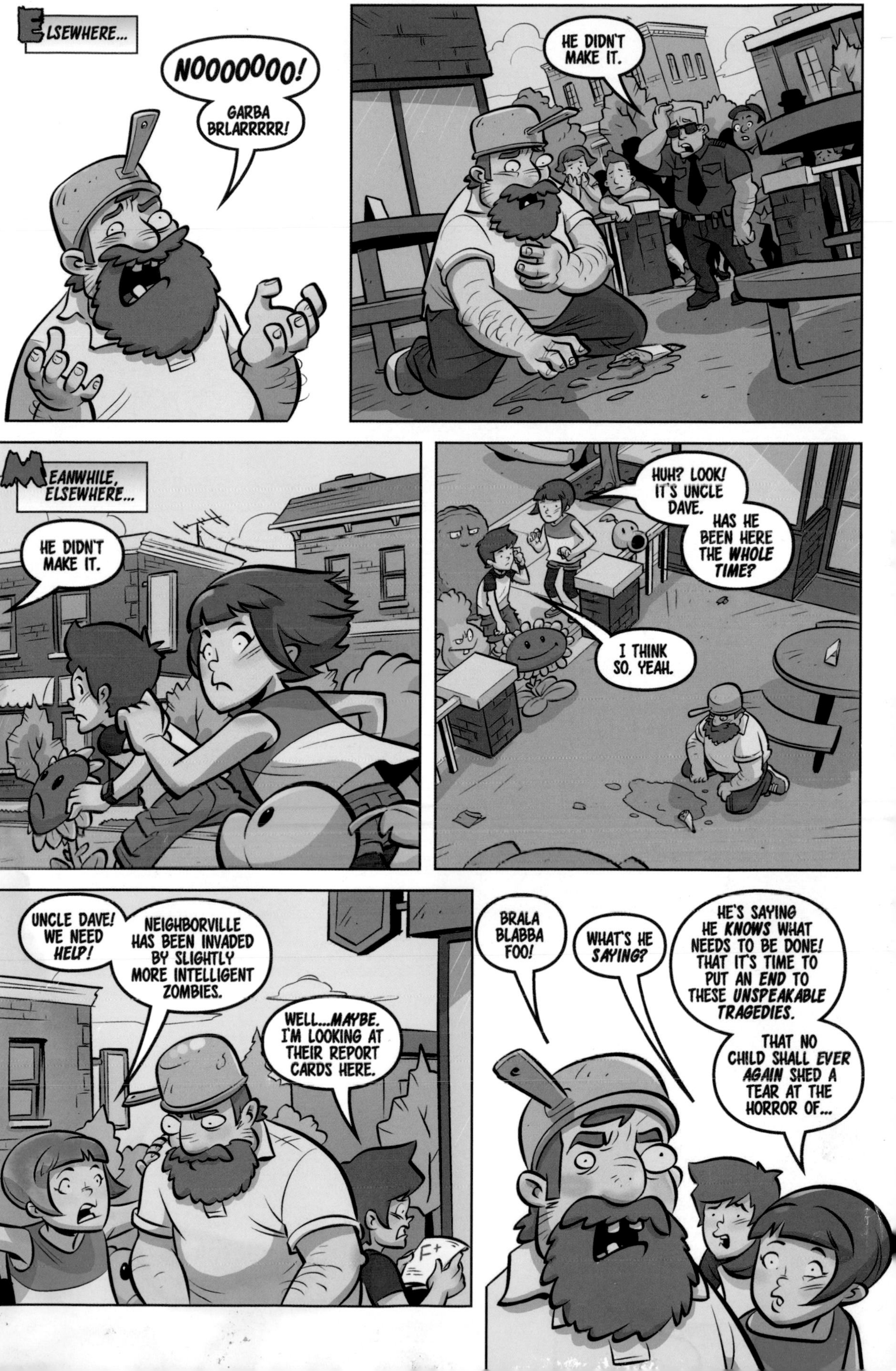
ELSEWHERE...
NOOOOOOO!
GARBA BRLARRRRR!
HE DIDN'T MAKE IT.
MEANWHILE, ELSEWHERE...
HE DIDN'T MAKE IT.
HUH? LOOK! IT'S UNCLE DAVE.
HAS HE BEEN HERE THE WHOLE TIME?
I THINK SO, YEAH.
UNCLE DAVE! WE NEED HELP!
NEIGHBORVILLE HAS BEEN INVADED BY SLIGHTLY MORE INTELLIGENT ZOMBIES.
WELL...MAYBE. I'M LOOKING AT THEIR REPORT CARDS HERE.
F+
BRALA BLABBA FOO!
WHAT'S HE SAYING?
HE'S SAYING HE KNOWS WHAT NEEDS TO BE DONE! THAT IT'S TIME TO PUT AN END TO THESE UNSPEAKABLE TRAGEDIES.
THAT NO CHILD SHALL EVER AGAIN SHED A TEAR AT THE HORROR OF...

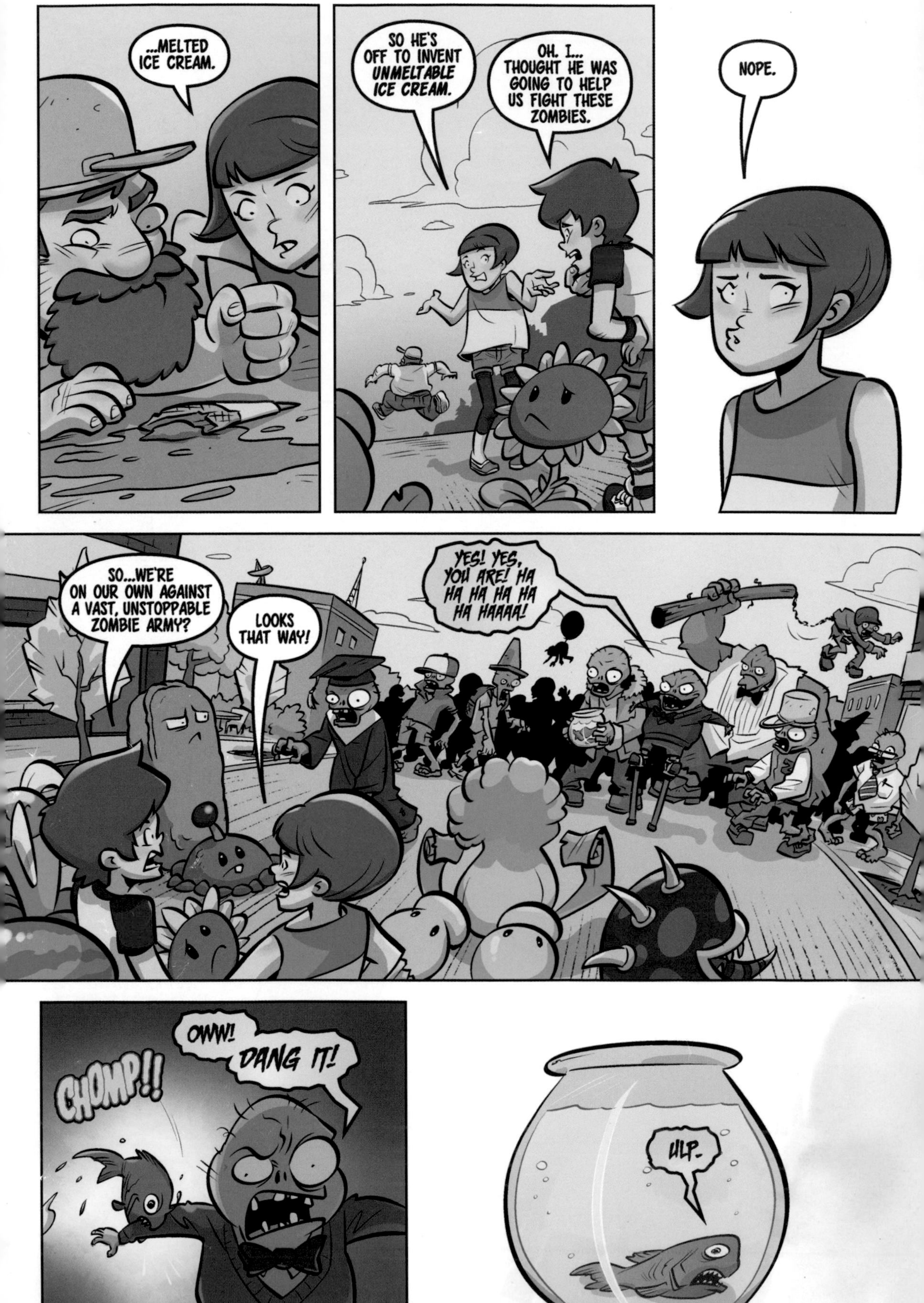
...MELTED ICE CREAM.
SO HE'S OFF TO INVENT *UNMELTABLE* ICE CREAM.
OH. I... THOUGHT HE WAS GOING TO HELP US FIGHT THESE ZOMBIES.
NOPE.
SO...WE'RE ON OUR OWN AGAINST A VAST, UNSTOPPABLE ZOMBIE ARMY?
LOOKS THAT WAY!
YES! YES, YOU ARE! HA HA HA HA HA HA HAAAA!
CHOMP!!
OWW!
DANG IT!
ULP.